GETS LOST AND FOUND
by Jill Kingdon

ILLUSTRATIONS BY

Delair

At last the big day was here and Dizzy could hardly believe it. He'd waited all year for the Carnivore Carnival to come to town. Dizzy, his mother and his father were the very first ones in line when the gates opened.

"Hurray! Hurray!" Dizzy called as he ran inside. "Mom! Dad! Look at all the rides. I'm going on them all!" And he charged ahead.

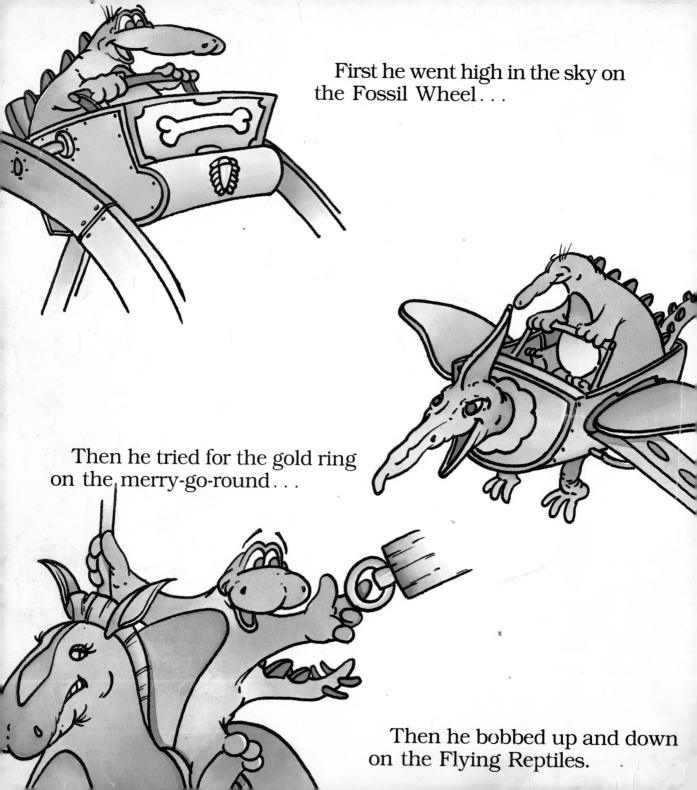

First he went high in the sky on the Fossil Wheel . . .

Then he tried for the gold ring on the merry-go-round . . .

Then he bobbed up and down on the Flying Reptiles.

After each ride he'd dash to the next. His mom and dad were having trouble keeping up with him. "Dizzy! Dizzy!" Dr. Dinosaur called. "You'll get lost. We can't keep up with you."

"Oh, Daddy, I won't get lost." And off he ran, quick as a wink.

Dr. and Mrs. Dinosaur tried very hard to stay with Dizzy, but the crowd was getting bigger and he ran so fast! Pretty soon they weren't behind him anymore.

"Hey, Dad. I'm hungry. Would you buy me some Swamp Sweets?"

"Dad . . . ? Mom? Where are you?" But no Mom or Dad answered. "Hmmm. Where could they have gotten to?"

"They should have stayed with me," Dizzy said, feeling a little annoyed but trying to be brave. "Oh, well. I'd better look for them."

So Dizzy started looking. "Maybe they went in there. I think I'll check."

But the Fun House turned out not to be fun at all.

Dizzy came out scared – and now he was crying.

"Hey, little one. Are you lost?" the Fun House
man asked. "What's your name?"
"I don't know," Dizzy cried, and began his
search again.

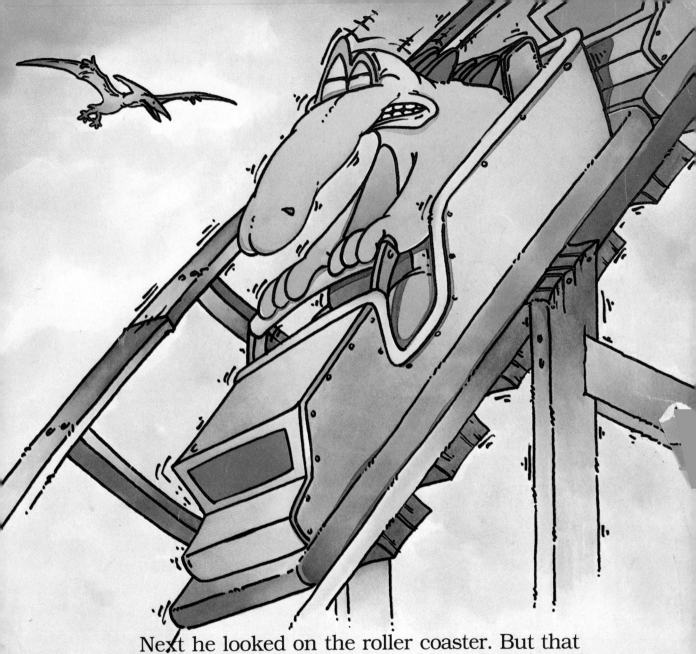

Next he looked on the roller coaster. But that was even more scary than the Fun House! And even if his mother and father were on it, he wouldn't have seen them because he was too frightened to open his eyes.

As he jumped off, Dizzy was looking sadder than ever.

"What's the matter, kid?" the roller coaster man asked. "Are you lost? I'll call your parents and have them come get you. What's your phone number?"

"I don't now!" wailed Dizzy. And he ran away.

In a few minutes he came to a ride called the Whip which a lot of grownups seemed to be going on. "Maybe they're on this one," he thought and hopped on.

But this was the
scariest ride so far.

Dizzy was very glad when it stopped. Still there was no sign of his parents. A tattooed tyrannosaurus helped him off and he said, "You look too young to be on this ride alone. Are you lost? Tell me your address, and I'll take you home."

"I don't know it!" screamed Dizzy and ran away before the tyrannosaurus could stop him.

Luckily for Dizzy, he ran straight into a policeman. "Hey, hey, not so fast. Where do you think you're going, young fella?"

"I'm lost," said Dizzy. "My mom and dad lost me."

"Well," said the policeman, "don't worry. We'll find them. Now, what's your name?"

"Dizzy," said Dizzy.

"And what's your last name?" asked the policeman.
"Dizzy," said Dizzy.
"Uh oh. It seems you don't know your last name. Well then, what's your address? Where do you live?" asked the policeman gently.

"In my house," answered Dizzy.
"But where is your house?" the policeman said.
"I'm not sure. I think you turn right and then left," replied Dizzy hopefully.

"Uh oh. I guess you don't know your address either. Well, what's your phone number?"

"Phone number? Um, I'm afraid I don't know that. But if you call my mom *she'll* tell you," said Dizzy, thinking he'd solved the problem.

Just then, the Fun House man, who'd been chasing Dizzy for some time, ran up, huffing and puffing. "He doesn't know his name," he told the policeman.

"Or his phone number," said the roller coaster man as he joined them. "Or his address," added the tattooed tyrannosaurus, screeching to a stop in the center of the group.

Everyone looked worried. Dizzy cried very loudly. The crowd surrounding him was growing and growing.

Just then, Dr. and Mrs. Dinosaur saw the crowd that was forming and heard a very familar sound. They ran over, pushed their way to the front and found their very own Dizzy!

"Oh, Dizzy. We were so frightened. We couldn't find you anywhere," said Mrs. Dinosaur.

"Well," said the policeman, "it's a good thing you did find him, because he doesn't know his name, his address or his phone number, so we would have had a hard time finding you!"

"I know," said Dr. Dinosaur meekly. "We've tried teaching him, but he can never remember."

"Gee," said the tattooed tyrannosaurus, "I always used to forget things too. But my father taught me to make up rhymes and they helped me remember."

"Come to think of it, that also worked for Dizzy," said Mrs. Dinosaur. She thought for a moment and said, "Okay, Dizzy, try this:

My name is Dizzy Dinosaur;
I live on Old Swamp Drive.
My house number is fifty-four;
My phone – six, two, one, five."

And sure enough, Dizzy remembered his name, address and phone number from then on.

The next day at school, Dizzy told his classmates about how he got lost at the Carnivore Carnival and how he learned his name, address and phone number.

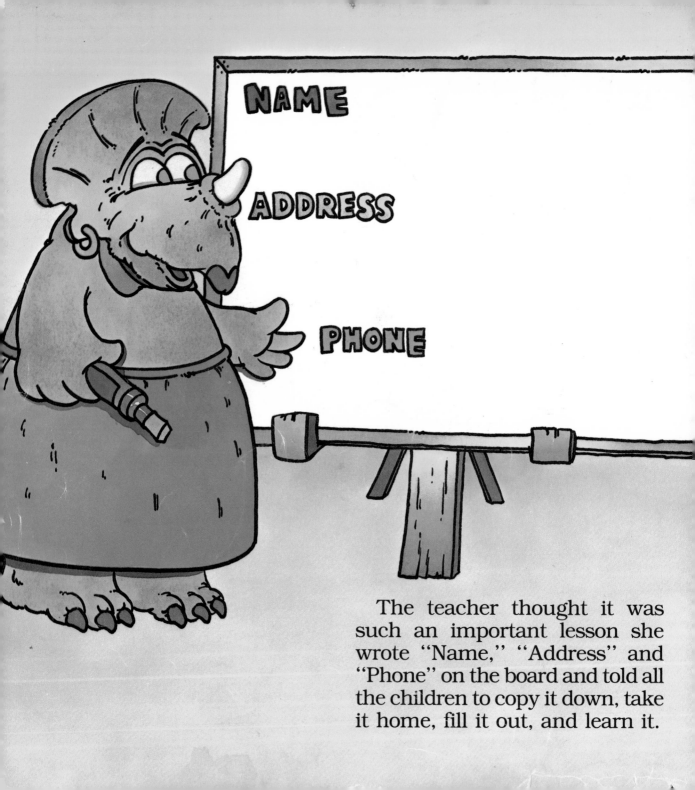

The teacher thought it was such an important lesson she wrote "Name," "Address" and "Phone" on the board and told all the children to copy it down, take it home, fill it out, and learn it.

"After all," she said, "if you ever get lost, you want to be sure you'll be found!"

Dizzy Dinosaur is a stegosaurus (you pronounce it: steg-o-SAWR-us). The stegosaurus was a plant-eating dinosaur which was very long and heavier than a car. But its head was quite small and its brain was the size of a walnut. (Maybe that's why Dizzy is so dizzy!) Any enemy who tried to bite the stegosaurus got a very unpleasant surprise: The stegosaurus had two rows of bony triangles going down his backbone and each triangle was as tall as a three-year-old child!